JACK'S TIME MACHINE

DAN JAMES

Troll

BridgeWater Books

For four precious children from my own time,
Carly, Liam, Lewis, and Matthew

WELCOME!

Y ou're about to enter a strange and mysterious world, where you'll meet a boy named Jack and a dog named Scruff. You'll travel with them across time and space, to the ancient and dangerous land of the Aztecs. There, Jack will risk his life to rescue a valuable treasure from a crafty fortune hunter, as he and Scruff try to make their way back home.

Jack's daring quest will lead him through a series of cunning traps, set by the Aztecs to protect their treasures. To make his way past these traps, he must solve five challenging puzzles. There are clues provided in the story, and in the pictures, too. As you share Jack's breathtaking adventure, study these hidden clues carefully, and see if you can discover the correct answers and the route that will bring Jack and Scruff to safety.

Try to figure out the puzzles on your own. But if you need extra help, the solutions are on page 32. Good luck in *Jack's Time Machine*!

It was just before Christmas, and Jack was spending the day with his grandfather. Grandpa enjoyed looking at old books, and he was usually full of exciting stories about faraway places and buried treasure.

Jack thought he might prefer to stay home, playing around on his computer, but his mother had said, "You'll have fun. You can put up some Christmas decorations for him. And you know you like playing with Scruff."

Scruff was Grandpa's dog. He was a cairn terrier, bright-eyed and intelligent. Scruff, Grandpa claimed, knew more about things than anyone dreamed possible.

Snow was falling thick and fast outside Grandpa's small house as Jack started to hang the ornaments and lights. Grandpa hadn't noticed. He was squinting at the small print in his book.

"I can't read this with my bad eyes," he grumbled. "Where are my glasses?" He looked up at Jack on the stepladder. "Can you see them from up there, Jack?"

Jack looked around the room, which was getting darker as the snow began to fall more thickly. No glasses. Grandpa shut the book. "What are you reading about, Grandpa?" asked Jack.

"I'll give you some clues, Jack," said Grandpa with a grin. "They were people who lived in Mexico around five hundred years ago. They built pyramids and had never seen horses."

"The Incas!" cried Jack.

"Mmm — not quite. They also loved to make things out of gold. Well, that was until Cortés and his soldiers started stealing it all. I wish just one of those thieves had been taught a lesson."

Jack sat at the top of the stepladder and studied a plastic star. "Did they have things like this in real gold?"

"The purest, yellowest gold you ever saw . . . And their main city was built on an island in a lake, in what is now the middle of Mexico City. . . . And . . ." Grandpa was deliberately speaking slowly to give Jack time to guess.

"AZTECS!" shouted Jack as the clock rang out. How many chimes, Jack couldn't count. "Well? Am I right?" he demanded over the noise of Scruff's barking. His grandfather was strangely silent.

"Grandpa?" gasped Jack. He edged slowly down the creaking stepladder. His grandfather didn't move. His finger was pointing into the air as if he were made of stone. Scruff whimpered and licked the old man's hand.

"Grandpa?" Jack's voice trembled. He wanted to shake him but didn't dare. Something about the frozen smile and staring eyes held him back. Why was it so quiet? Jack looked fearfully around the room. The clock had stopped, both hands pointing to twelve. Jack looked out the window. The snow hung motionless, like on a Christmas card. Jack flung open the window and picked a flake out of the air. He watched it melt on his palm. He quickly shut the window again.

"This is really scary, Scruff," he muttered. "What should I do?"

Suddenly the clock door creaked open. Jack could hardly bear to look at it. If there was someone there, why didn't Scruff bark? "Go get it, Scruff," he hissed, whirling around.

Scruff wagged his tail and sniffed the clock, pushing the door wider still.

Jack tiptoed over and looked in. There on a small shelf were Grandpa's glasses. As Jack's eyes got used to the gloom, he saw that the inside of the clock was covered in astronomical drawings and calculations. He climbed in to get a better look.

The back of the clock face was the strangest part of all. It had a lever pointing to the word HOME. The rest of the circle was covered with tiny paintings. Scruff jumped in beside Jack and sat down panting. He was obviously waiting for something to happen. "What do I do, Scruff?" asked Jack, feeling more excited than scared now. "Move the lever? Should I try it?" Scruff wagged his tail.

Jack gripped the lever with both hands and pushed it in a counterclockwise

 direction. Nothing happened. He pushed harder. The lever creaked, and as it began to move, the clock clicked and whirred. The end of the lever passed the pictures of the Roman temple and the Vikings. Now Jack couldn't stop it. It slid past the highwayman and

the pyramids of Egypt, and on to some buildings Jack didn't recognize. Then, with a loud click and a shudder, it stopped. The clock door slammed shut. Scruff yelped as an ear-splitting chime rattled the woodwork and Jack's head.

The clock swayed violently from left to right, up and down. Jack's head was filled with babbling voices speaking hundreds of strange languages. He jammed his back against one side of the clock and his hands against the opposite side. "HOLD ON TIGHT!" he yelled to Scruff. At the sixth chime, the clock stopped short. Jack slumped to the floor, and Scruff licked his face.

"Are you all right, Scruff?" Jack asked nervously. Scruff licked his face again, then pushed his nose against the clock door. It opened gently to reveal not Grandpa's old, worn carpet, but dry ground and stones.

"What — where are we?" wondered Jack, scrambling to his feet. Somewhere outside, a dog barked. It was sunset, but it was as hot as a summer's day.

"Is this a dream?" Jack frowned and stepped out of the clock. Now he could hear the sound of far-off drums and chanting voices. In the distance, a huge pyramid loomed out of the dim light. Flickering torches danced like fireflies.

"I think it's Mexico, Scruff. We're in M-Mexico — in Aztec times!"

9

A slight rustling noise made Jack swing around. He just had time to notice that the clock had landed in front of a huge temple-like building when a clammy hand was clamped over his mouth. Jack felt himself being dragged across the ground, up some steps, and into the doorway of the temple.

Scruff yelped and snarled. Then a voice hissed in Jack's ear. "Silence your dog before I do, or the savages will kill both of us."

"Shush, Scruff, good boy," soothed Jack, looking fearfully at the razor-sharp knife his abductor held in his other hand. Jack grabbed Scruff's collar. The stranger pulled them back into the shadows behind a pillar, just as a group of men rushed past the temple and up to the clock. They were wearing very few clothes and elaborate masks. Jack watched in dismay as the Aztecs — for that is what they were — began to dance around the clock, chanting. Then four men lifted it up. Jack knew he had to stop them. He struggled, kicked, and squirmed to get away from the grasp of his captor, who was whispering to him, "They think your box is the chariot of a god returning to rescue them." Jack gasped as the chanting Aztecs solemnly marched off, bearing the clock toward the pyramid.

"Hey! That's my grandpa's clock!" he yelled. *And my only means of escape*, he thought desperately. But too late — the clock and the Aztecs had disappeared into the rays of the setting sun.

"Shhh, boy! They will have taken it to the Temple of the Moon. Don't panic."

All very well for him, thought Jack. "Who are you? Let me go!" he demanded.

The tall, thin man raised his chin, swept his cloak over his shoulder, and twiddled each end of his waxed mustache.

"I am Don Juan de Valdez," he said arrogantly. "I am pleased to make your acquaintance. I am certain we can help each other."

 Jack felt uneasy. He looked at Scruff, who was snarling under his breath. Could they trust Valdez?

"Look, boy, I saved your life, didn't I?" said Valdez  impatiently, his eyes narrowing to slits as he waved his dagger before Jack's face.

"Well, I suppose . . ." Jack said cautiously.

"Good!" cried Valdez. "Now, you assist me in a small matter, and I will help you get your granny's bell box back — *si*? Where did you come from anyway, boy? I was busy retrieving *my* gold star from these mindless, thieving savages. The next thing I knew there was an enormous flash, and there you were drawing attention to both of us. It is lucky for you that I was here, or they would have eaten you alive!"

Jack didn't believe a word. It was clear who the thief was here.

"Now, if you get the star from behind that door for me, I will show you a secret passage to the Temple of the Moon, where your precious clock has been taken. *Comprende*?" Valdez continued.

Jack gulped and nodded in agreement, while Scruff continued to growl.

"Go, go, then, boy," ordered Valdez, waving his dagger once more. "The star rests in the chest of the Aztec sun-god statue over there."

For the first time, Jack looked up. They were standing outside the entrance to the Temple of the Sun.

It was guarded by a massive wooden portcullis. In front of it were a number of raised stones arranged in a circle.

"When you stand on the correct stone, the gate will rise," explained Valdez. Jack looked up. Above the stones was a deadly array of sharp spikes.

"What happens if I stand on the wrong stone?" Jack asked, although he could guess the answer. Valdez came over and dug his nails into Jack's shoulder until it began to hurt.

"If you stand on the wrong stone," he said, "you will die."

Jack saw that he had no alternative. He felt beads of sweat on his forehead. He could just glimpse the gold through the doorway. Then he looked down at the eight raised stones. Each one was painted a different color, and in the center was a large carved picture of the sun god.

"Come on, hurry up!" Valdez urged him.

Jack looked up at the spikes again. His heart pounded. The colors were confusing. He couldn't think straight.

Concentrate . . . he said to himself. He knelt down and put his arm around Scruff's neck. The dog licked his nose. Calmer now, Jack thought hard. Then he stood up and stepped on one of the stones. There was a deep rumbling under the floor, and the spikes above him shuddered. The portcullis creaked and slowly began to rise. Jack felt a sudden thrill of excitement. He had done it! In front of him was the statue, and resting on its chest was the most beautiful gold star he had ever seen.

"The gold, boy — GET THE GOLD!" shouted Valdez. Jack leaped off the stone and dashed into the temple. Reaching up on tiptoe, he managed to grasp the star, but as he did so, the portcullis began to close behind him.

WHICH **COLOR** DOESN'T BELONG? WILL JACK SEE THE **LIGHT**?

"Hurry!" screamed Valdez. Too late. With a grinding thud, the gate hit the ground. Jack was frozen in terror, but Valdez thrust his hand through a gap in the timbers. "Give me the star, and I'll stand on the stone. Then you'll be free."

Jack didn't trust Valdez and he hesitated. The hand disappeared. "I won't stand on the stone *unless* you give me the star," Valdez threatened. He thrust his hand through again. "Put the star in this bag!"

Jack suddenly became angry, and his mind was icy clear. Valdez didn't have all the answers.

"And you'll tell me how to get my clock back, won't you?" Jack asked coldly, passing the bag with something inside it back to Valdez.

Valdez snatched the bag. "Yes, of course, of course," he said. Then Jack heard his gloating laugh as his footsteps disappeared down the temple steps.

Jack took the gold star from his pocket and looked at it. It glinted in the dim light of the passageway and felt heavy in his hand. His watch beeped — it was still going. What would Valdez do when he discovered the plastic Christmas star Jack had put in the bag instead?

Torchlight flickered through the cracks in the portcullis and faintly lit the interior of the temple. All was quiet. A snake slithered across the floor and disappeared.

The walls, Jack could now see, were covered with pictures and symbols carved into the stone. He listened through the gate. There was no sound. How much time would he have before Valdez found out that he had been tricked? He rubbed some of the dust away from the pictures. Those on one wall seemed to tell a story. There were images of a fair-skinned god and a tall box. "Just like me with Grandpa's clock," gasped Jack. On the next wall were scenes of Aztec people. On the last wall was a plan of the temple he was in. It showed that,

farther along, several tunnels led from the temple to other places. Most of them dropped into deep pits with snakes and other deadly traps. Just one route led through several different chambers to the Temple of the Moon.

"That's where Valdez said the Aztecs would take the clock!" exclaimed Jack. Scruff wagged his tail.

In a torchlit corner Jack discovered entrances to five different tunnels. One of them was the tunnel he needed, but which one? Above the entrances were several symbols. Jack studied the wall. If he could solve the puzzle, perhaps he could get his clock back without help from Valdez. He hardly heard Scruff's warning growl.

"What is it, boy?" Jack asked, but then he nearly jumped out of his skin.

"It's your old friend Valdez," hissed a familiar voice from outside the portcullis. "I believe you have something of mine. . . ."

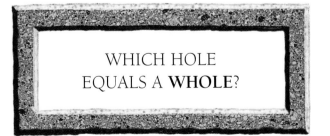

WHICH HOLE
EQUALS A **WHOLE**?

Valdez jumped onto the raised stone that Jack had stood on earlier. The stone sank, and the floor rumbled. The portcullis started to rise, and Valdez began to squeeze underneath, but he moved too fast. As his feet left the stone, it jerked up and the wooden spikes of the portcullis banged down, trapping Valdez by the back of his pants.

In a flash, Jack understood the solution to the puzzle. With Scruff in his arms, he jumped into one of the holes, gritting his teeth as they slid down the twisting tunnel. They landed on a pile of straw at the end of another dimly lit passage. With one hand on Scruff's collar, Jack felt his way along the tunnel wall, stumbling ahead until he reached an open chamber. They were greeted by a horrifying sight. A thousand rotting human heads were stacked high along the chamber walls. This was the Temple of Skulls. Jack felt sick.

Scruff didn't like it either. He whimpered and pawed the ground. Jack looked down and saw that, instead of solid floor, the bottom of the chamber was a swampy pool. Three slimy stone columns rose above the water like three huge stepping stones. Jack backed toward the door and stopped short. He heard a muffled thud, followed by a stream of curses from the other end of the tunnel. Valdez was coming.

Jack looked across the pool. On the far side was a doorway, but how could he reach it? He leaped from the side of the pool to the first stone, but the next one was too far to jump to. He looked wildly around the room. Valdez's stumbling footsteps were getting louder. By the entrance were two pairs of strong wooden stilts. Jack picked up a pair and lowered them into the water. Then he climbed onto them. Even if he could manage the stilts, how would he get Scruff across? "Come on, boy!" he called. "Swim!" Scruff sprang onto one of the stones, then gazed down at the water. Jack carefully moved one stilt forward. The dog whined

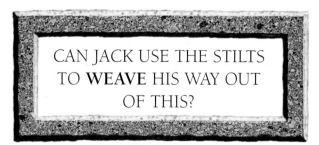

CAN JACK USE THE STILTS
TO **WEAVE** HIS WAY OUT
OF THIS?

anxiously. Suddenly the water parted, and Jack saw two huge rows of sharp, shiny teeth! "Yikes! It's an alligator!" The animal's massive jaws snapped shut on the end of one of the stilts. Jack and Scruff jumped backward into the doorway as the stilt broke in two. "There must be another way," Jack said.

He grabbed the remaining stilts and hopped back onto the first stone, cringing as a skeleton slipped down into the water. Scruff jumped up behind him. Jack pushed one of the stilts toward the next stone. Perhaps he could form a bridge. "It's too short!" he exclaimed. Then something Grandpa had told him long ago started coming back to him. "I think I've got it!" he whispered, picking up the stilt and setting to work.

Valdez was so close that Jack could hear him muttering.

He picked up Scruff and crossed the pool to the stone nearest the exit tunnel. All he had to do now was pull one stilt along to make a bridge between the stone and the edge of the pool. The other stilts fell into the water below and drifted back to the far side. Jack was glad that Valdez would not see how he had done it. As he ran down the next tunnel, he thought of the alligator lurking in the pool and shuddered. "They deserve each other!" he muttered to Scruff.

The tunnel was lit by flaming torches. Scruff trotted on ahead, and Jack ran after him, around a long sweeping bend to the left. It led into a chamber with a wooden floor. Jack could hear the wind howling somewhere far below. His footsteps sounded hollow, as though a vast empty nothingness lay beneath the floor. The room too was completely empty, except for a row of levers with strange markings on them. Across the room was a doorway, blocked by a solid slab of stone.

Jack peered at the squiggles on the levers. *It must be Aztec writing — or numbers — or something!* he thought. He wasn't at all sure which. "What do they mean,

Scruff?" Jack asked desperately. Scruff shook his head and sneezed. He sat down by the entrance to the chamber, on the lookout for Valdez. A heavy stone slab hung high above his head.

Jack looked again at the symbols. They had to

18

mean something. It was clear that the levers opened one door and closed the other.

Jack thought hard for several minutes. He was sure that the order in which the levers were lowered was the key, but which one came first? He glanced at Scruff. The dog was panting but not agitated. No sign of Valdez yet.

"Well, here goes, Scruff." Jack began to lower the levers one by one. "Don't sit too near the door, boy, or it might come down on top of you." Scruff whined, took a few steps back, and sat down again. Jack wiped the sweat from his forehead and pulled another lever. As the last lever clunked into place, the heavy stone slab came down with a deafening crash, blocking off the tunnel behind them.

"Now the other door should open," Jack told Scruff. The door didn't move, but the floor jerked and began a very slow, grinding journey away from the levers and into the far wall. A freezing wind roared up through the widening gap. Jack's hair stood on end as he looked into the bottomless chasm.

Scruff started barking and jumped at the closed door of the tunnel, but that escape route was blocked. Jack's feet were gradually getting farther away from the levers. Soon he would have to let go of the levers, or fall into the hole.

"Quiet, boy," he yelled at Scruff. "I have to think. . . ."

The wind howled, buffeting Jack as he fought to keep his mind on the symbols. He quickly lifted all the levers. The floor shuddered but continued to move. Jack looked carefully at each symbol in turn.

"Yes!" cried Jack. "I've got it now!" He began to pull down the levers one by one. The floor still edged away. As Jack pulled the last lever, he had to stretch so far across the gap that he couldn't push himself upright again. If this didn't work, he had had it for sure. CLLLUUUNKKK! The floor jolted to a standstill. Jack still couldn't move. There was another jolt, and the floor began to slide back toward the levers. His body slowly rose upright again, but he didn't let go of the last lever until the floor had touched the wall. The cold wind disappeared and became again like a distant howl below his feet.

After a moment's silence, both doors rumbled and lifted. What a relief! The feeling didn't last long, however. In the distance, wet footsteps could be heard staggering along the tunnel.

"Oh, no!" cried Jack. "Come on, Scruff. Let's get out of here!"

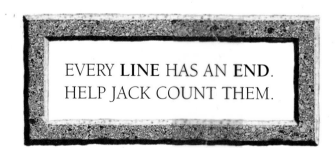

EVERY **LINE** HAS AN **END**.
HELP JACK COUNT THEM.

"Wait!" gasped Valdez, who had managed to escape the jaws of the alligator with the help of the stilts and his sharp dagger. "Wait for me! I won't hurt you! Let's go together!" He stumbled after them, his clothes tattered and torn and dripping with water.

But Jack and Scruff had already disappeared through the doorway in the far wall. A stairway stretched before them, first long and straight, then curving around and around in a seemingly endless spiral. Jack held Scruff's collar, and the dog helped pull him up more than four hundred steps. At last, panting and thirsty, they reached moonlight and the Temple of the Moon.

On the other side of the thick stone wall, voices were singing in a low, monotonous tone. The Aztecs!

"I bet that's Grandpa's clock they're chanting to," whispered Jack. "But we've still got to find a way through that wall before we can get it back."

He looked around. There were no tunnels this time. He looked up. High up, out of reach, were four door-sized holes in the wall. And in front of the wall were four thick, springy timbers, tied down with rope to four rings set in the floor.

Hmmm. Giant catapults, thought Jack. If he clung to one of the wooden timbers and cut the rope, it would shoot him through the hole in the wall. "Why four holes?" he wondered, but he knew the answer. Three would lead to disaster — and the fourth? Would it lead straight into the arms of the Aztecs? Would they be so amazed he'd escaped their traps that they'd let him have his clock back?

Jack sighed. There was no other way out — he'd have to solve this puzzle, too. More eerie engravings covered the walls. One panel in particular caught Jack's attention, and he walked up to look at it more closely.

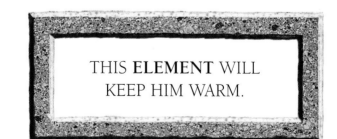

THIS **ELEMENT** WILL
KEEP HIM WARM.

The panel showed four square boxes and three simple pictures. The fourth box was empty. On the floor under the springy wooden timbers were four more drawings, one for each timber.

"One of these drawings fits into that empty box, Scruff. But which one?" As Jack leaned backward against the wall to think, he fell into a hidden alcove. There on the floor lay a large coil of rope. A solution began to form in Jack's mind. He took out a penknife and opened up one of the blades, hoping it was sharp enough to cut the rope. Valdez certainly had a sharp enough knife. Valdez! He'd almost forgotten about him! Grandpa's voice came back to him: "I wish just one of those thieves had been taught a lesson!" That gave Jack an idea.

"Why don't they wait for me?" cried Valdez as he climbed the long staircase. "When I get my hands on them, I'll make them pay for this!" Eventually, he reached the last step. Jack was nowhere in sight. All that remained was a length of rope hanging from one of the holes high up on the wall.

"So, boy . . . you think I am not as clever as you?" cried Valdez. "Not so! It is you who are the fool. All you had to do was hang on to the timber, like so," he said, clambering on and wrapping an arm about one of the catapults. "Then, take a sharp knife, like so," he added, slicing the razor-sharp blade to and fro against the rope. "And finally, cut the rope in two like . . ."

"So?" enquired Jack, stepping out from the dark recess with Scruff at his feet.

"Yes, exactly! Like — WHAAAT!" Valdez's reply became a scream as the last strands of rope parted company.

"See you around, Valdez!" said Jack, as the Spaniard hurtled through the hole in the wall, his screams trailing after him. "I told you throwing the rope through the wrong hole would fool him, Scruff!"

The chanting stopped. Jack heard the Aztecs shout, "The cage! A prisoner in the cage!" and the sound of running feet on the other side of the wall.

"Now's our chance, Scruff, while they're distracted by Valdez. Let's go." He picked Scruff up, jumped onto one of the other timbers, and began to cut the rope.

25

With a snap the timber
flew into the air, and Jack and Scruff
hurtled through the window. They landed
hard at the top of a steep stairway. Breathless
and dizzy, they scrambled down the stairs,
tripping over the last few steps and tumbling to a
stop at the feet of a frail old man. His hair was long
and matted, and looking at his special headdress,
Jack was sure he was a priest.

The priest peered at Jack and then at Valdez, who was
trapped in a cage, suspended high above the floor.

"More Spaniards, I suppose — trying to steal our gold!" said
the priest.

"No, no, not me — him!" cried Valdez and Jack at the same time. A tall, strong
Aztec with a spear moved closer to Jack, guarding him.

"Look," wheedled Valdez. "I have a present for
you. Something more precious than gold." He held
out the plastic star Jack had put in his bag. "Take it.
Feel how little it weighs!"

26

He dropped the star, and one of the Aztecs retrieved it and carried it to the priest. The old man felt the ornament and held it up with his arms outstretched. The Aztecs sighed.

"Where did this come from?" asked the priest.

"Why, from the gods, of course!" replied Valdez cunningly. "If you set me free, I promise you many more gifts."

The priest nodded, and an Aztec warrior moved over to untie the rope that held the cage.

"He's lying!" cried Jack. "Don't believe him!"

The priest had almost forgotten about Jack. Now he swung around. "Who are you?"

"He's a thief!" shouted Valdez. "Search him. He's got your gold star. Get me down — I'll show you." Valdez shook the cage door. The Aztecs murmured angrily.

"SILENCE!" the priest commanded. He looked at Jack's pale skin. "Are you a god, too?" he asked.

"I'm not a god and he's not a god." Jack pointed to Valdez and hurriedly tried to explain. "He was going to steal your star. Look, here it is. Take it." He thrust the gold star into the old man's hands.

At that moment, Jack's watch beeped again to mark the hour. The priest jumped in surprise, then grabbed Jack's wrist and peered at the dial.

"What is this squeaking thing? Is it alive?"

"No." Jack smiled. "It's a watch. It measures time — like that one." He pointed to the grandfather clock, which now stood alone in the middle of the floor. The priest looked at the clock face and then back at Jack. "You came in the chariot — YOU ARE A GOD!" he cried, and dropped flat on the floor in front of Jack. The other Aztecs stretched out their arms and fell to the floor, too, chanting softly.

Valdez was furious. He rattled the cage and shouted, "He's not a god, you idiots! He's just a boy."

Jack knelt down beside the old man. "Can I go now, please? You have your star back, and Grandpa will be worried about me."

The priest took Jack's hand and looked closely at the watch. The way he squinted reminded Jack of his grandpa without his glasses.

That's it! he thought. *The old man has bad eyesight!*

He ran over to the clock and grabbed Grandpa's glasses from the little shelf inside.

"Here," he said to the priest, who was slowly getting to his feet, "try these." He slipped the glasses onto the old man's nose. The priest opened his eyes and looked all around him. He looked at his own hands and then at Jack. He slowly raised his arms toward the sky.

"I can see!" he cried.

The Aztecs cheered and bowed to Jack. Their prayers, it seemed, had been answered. "Now I really must go," Jack insisted.

The priest nodded and held out the gold star. "Take this with you," he said with a beaming smile. "It is a gift from us to the gods."

Jack grasped the shining gold star in his hands. What would Grandpa say when he saw this? He removed his quartz watch and offered it to the priest. "Please keep this — if you would like it," he said, and climbed into the clock, eagerly followed by Scruff.

"Don't leave me in here," shouted Valdez. Jack remembered his grandfather's stories about what the Aztecs did to their prisoners and hesitated. His hand was already on the lever, but he let go of it and stepped out of the clock again.

"What about him?" he asked the priest, who was now proudly wearing the watch and glasses. "You're not going to sacrifi —"

"No, no," whispered the priest. "It would annoy Cortés too much. But we'll leave him up there a bit longer, just to teach him a lesson!"

Jack grinned and jumped back into the clock. "Bye!" he yelled, and pushed the

 lever around to HOME. As the door slammed shut, the clock rang loudly and shuddered to life once more. After six deafening chimes, the clock came to a halt and the door burst open. Jack and Scruff were home again, in Grandpa's living room.

What a relief! thought Jack. Scruff jumped out of the clock wagging his tail.

Grandpa was just as they had left him, pointing his finger toward the top of the stepladder. The snow still hung in the air.

"Grandpa?" Jack prodded him gently, but the old man could not hear a word. "Wake up, Grandpa!" Jack yelled. Nothing.

Scruff licked Grandpa's hand, then lay down at his feet in exactly the same position he had been in when time stood still.

"Oh, I see," said Jack. He climbed to the top of the stepladder and pulled some string and his penknife out of his pocket. But what about the star? There was only one thing to do. He tapped the gold star and took a deep breath. He looked straight at Grandpa and shouted, "Aztecs!"

The clock door slammed shut, the pendulum began to swing again, and the clock ticked contentedly. The snow outside fell gently through the air.

"Well done, Jack!" cried Grandpa, jumping out of his chair. "Now let's see you put that star on the tree!"

Jack hesitated. Should he explain? No, he felt too tired to tell the whole story just now. He tied the star to the tree, but it was so heavy that its weight pulled the top right over. Jack hoped his grandfather wouldn't notice. Grandpa gazed up at the gleaming star.

"You know, Jack, without my glasses, that looks almost like real gold!" he said with a grin.

Jack yawned. Scruff was already fast asleep on the rug. "I'm just going to make a cup of tea," said Grandpa as Jack sank into a chair. "You rest awhile, and then you can tell me all about the Aztecs!"

MORE CLUES ARE IN THE
CHANGES TO THE PICTURE.

JACK'S SOLUTION PAGE

A rainbow of colors — but one color's wrong! (page 13)

In the Sun Temple, the carved center stone shows the face of an Aztec sun god. Jack has to select the correct colored outer stone to step on, to raise the wooden portcullis and avoid those spikes! White light and rainbows are made up of the spectrum of colors (red, orange, yellow, green, blue, indigo, violet). Which stone is the odd one out? The brown stone!

How can three moons make a moon whole? (page 15)

Jack has to pick the right tunnel to enter, and quickly! He does this by adding up the moon fractions painted above each hole. For instance, the left hole shows a whole moon, a quarter moon, and a half moon. Added together these equal one and three quarters. The hole on the right adds up to one (a whole) moon.

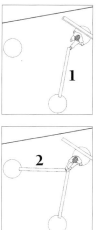

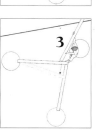

Weave the stilts under and over. (page 17)

To cross the pool, Jack makes a stable platform by interlocking three stilts. He picks up the stilts, jumps onto the nearest stone, and drops stilt number 1 into place. Holding this with his foot, he drops stilt number 2 into position and places it on his foot on top of 1. He then slides number 2 along and pushes number 3 under 1 and over 2.

Every line must have an end. Can you count them? (pages 19 and 21)

Jack manages to lower the levers in the correct order and reverse the sliding floor. How does he do it? The levers have symbols that reveal the order. Each of the symbols is made up of a number of lines. Counting the number of line *ends* gives each symbol a unique value from one to six.

Nature has lost an element! (pages 23 and 24)

A painted panel on the temple wall shows three different pictures and an empty space. On the floor under each of the four timbers is another picture. Only one of these four pictures on the floor depicts the correct subject to fit into the space on the wall panel. Each of the drawings on the wall represents one of the four elements of nature: Earth, Air, Fire, and Water. The missing element is Fire, so the third timber from the left is the one Jack needs!

More clues are in the changes to the picture. (pages 5 and 31)

1 Jack steps on the correct brown stone.
2 The book shows the whole moon.
3 Three sticks on top of the lampshade reveal how to make a stable platform.
4 The green ornament is now purple and reflects one of the lever symbols, as an example. Three small arrows point to the ends of the lines, and the number 3 shows its value.
5 The holiday card shows the missing Fire panel in place.